Pam & Johnny

Debra Hammond

American Literary Press, Inc.
Baltimore, Maryland

Pam & Johnny

Library of Congress
Cataloging in Publication Data
ISBN 1-56167-187-8

Printed by

American Literary Press

8019 Belair Road, Suite 10
Baltimore, Maryland

This book is dedicated to my family
for all their support,
and Diana for always being there.
Also in loving memory of Bertha B. Hammond
who will stay in our hearts forever.

CHAPTER 1

In a small quiet town called Amster, with shops up and down the boardwalk and the ocean meets the sand, my life changed. It happened three years ago. I remember it so clearly. It is a memory that I'll never forget.

It was a hot summer's day in June, and what a day it was. Everything seemed to be going well back then. I met a boy that I enjoyed being with (most of the time). His name was Brad. Looking back, maybe I spent a little too much time over his house. I probably could have been doing something more productive with my time.

While Brad was playing basketball with his friends, I stared at a little girl playing hopscotch. I could feel a presence nearby. I turned and couldn't believe what I saw! There was an incredible boy with dark hair, blue eyes and a radiant smile. What a man! Believe me I knew he was something special. His eyes pierced through me, like a wolf ready to pounce on his unsuspecting victim. When I looked into his eyes, I could see his inner warmth. I could see and feel what he was thinking. His sleek figure and strong hands could rip a man's heart right out of his chest. His lips could melt icy snow. He was a man of strength and stability. I couldn't believe the vision I beheld.

"Who is that ?" I asked in the middle of Brad's dunk shot.

Brad yelled "Johnny come over here, I want you to meet someone."

Johnny rushed over. He stood in front of me, it took every ounce of energy I had to keep my mouth from dropping open. He was incredible. His lips were so sensual and his eyes were like crystal blue pools of water from a still pond. I wanted to dive in. An unbelievable feeling shot through me like an arrow from an Indian's bow. A cool breeze went from my toes to the top of my head. It truly was the best feeling I'd ever felt.

I had to ignore this man, maybe for all the wrong reasons. Perhaps I was scared to leave Brad with a broken heart. Of course the fact that they were next door neighbors didn't help much.

I was afraid that I would never see this man again. I let some time go by and tried to get my feelings back to normal. Believe me it wasn't easy to try and forget someone like this. I was doing well for a while until the day I saw him walk out his front door. He was wearing blue jeans shorts, a plain tee shirt, and a baseball cap to match. The longer I stayed in my relationship with Brad, the more I wanted to be with Johnny. I felt trapped and lonely. I knew I didn't want to spend the rest of my life with the person I was with. It was three long years of nothing. Things were never good or bad, just uneventful. We never fought but we never had special time either. I had to make the first move, he surely wouldn't. He had no idea how strong my feelings were for him. For all he knew I was in love with Brad. We always put on a show, pretending that we were happy, things aren't always as they seem.

I knew that what I was about to do could ruin everything I had with Brad but, it was a chance I had to take. I couldn't spend my life just looking through a window. I had to think of the perfect way to express my feelings for him. If only I could get him alone but I couldn't pull him aside. Brad would be suspicious and run over in a flash. He'd want to know what we were talking about. My only solution was the old mail routine. I would write a brief letter. I couldn't take it anymore. I needed to get all of this emotion out. Maybe I could even send a rose along with the letter. The only problem was that I couldn't tell him who I was. I couldn't risk Brad finding out. In time I could tell Brad in my own way. He had to hear it from me first. There was so much at stake considering that Brad and Johnny were such good friends.

Later that night, when I was sure that I wouldn't be seen I slipped the letter and the rose into his screen door.

I was friendly with Johnny's sister Kate so getting into his house wasn't a problem at all. Kate was a tall girl with long flowing brown hair and the nicest smile. She was eager to give me a tour of the entire house. Brad's sister Jane came along even though she had been in the house many times before. I was anxious to find where the rose was, I had to know if it ended up in the right hands. Trying to remain calm but looking around the house in a state of panic, I tried to locate the rose. It wasn't in the kitchen, it wasn't in the living room, it wasn't even in his bedroom. Then

I saw it out of the corner of my eye. Red like a stocking on Christmas Eve. The petals glowing from the sun shining through the window. It was so open and full of life. It seemed more vibrant than when I bought it. As if it was taking it's first breath of air. Moisture dripped off the rose like melting ice cubes. It was in an extraordinary sparkling glass vase placed upon the television set. The rose was serving its purpose. It looked happy and loved, and that's exactly how I wanted Johnny to feel. I walked closer to the rose but stopped myself. I didn't want to look to suspicious.

I couldn't resist temptation I had to smell the sweet scent of the rose. As I cupped the petals in my hand and lowered my nose to breathe in its fragrance, Kate spoke.

"Someone sent Johnny that rose."

I tried not to blush, "Who?" I asked.

"Well, people seem to think that you sent it." Kate said.

I laughed nervously, "You're kidding, right?"

"No, I'm serious." Kate said.

"Why would I do that?"

"We've seen the way you stare at him" Kate said.

"What about Brad, he and I are so..." I could not finish the lie I was just about to tell. I didn't want to confuse Johnny.

Johnny paced nervously behind me.

"I didn't hear you come in" I said.

"Are you admiring my rose?" Johnny said.

"Yes it's beautiful!" I felt like I was going to choke.

"I'm going to find out who sent it to me." His tone became harsh. I panicked and blamed Jane. It was the only way out of it.

"Did you really send it to me?" Johnny asked.

Jane answered, "Yes I sent it."

We all laughed because Johnny was like a brother to Jane. He would never be interested in Jane and we all knew it.

Johnny started arguing with Kate to take a shower. They had plans to go out later and Kate always spent too much time getting ready. Johnny raised his voice and Kate started yelling. Jane and I decided to make an exit.

I was a little shaken up from my run in with Johnny but I had to forget and headed to work. It figures I had to work the hottest day of the summer. I'm sure I won't have many customers who will want to buy tapes and cd's on a day like this. My parents were at their vacation home, they had the right idea.

I'm sure they were at the beach swimming and sunbathing. It would have been good to be with them soaking up the rays. If only I could enjoy the weather. It was probably just as well that I had a job. I doubt I could fully enjoy the day considering all I could think about was Johnny. As soon as I got into work the phone rang. It was my mother,

"You're not going to believe who just stopped by." Mom said.

"Who?" I asked.

"Johnny Salve!"

"What's he doing down there?" I asked.

"Visiting his Aunt" Mom said.

"This is great. Now you can talk to him."

"What do you want me to tell him?" My mother asked.

"That I sent the rose." I replied.

"Are you sure?" Mom questioned.

I held in a deep breath and replied, "Yes!"

It wasn't easy trying to concentrate on work, I was pacing back and forth wondering what he would say when she told him. I was afraid but, I guess I had to know his reaction. Maybe this would be a step forward for us and we could be together. My mother called back in what seemed to be the longest two hours of my life.

"What happened?" I asked.

"Well, he was quite surprised. He really thought that you and Brad were happy together. He had no idea that things weren't going well."

"Did he seem interested?" I asked.

"He asked me a bunch of questions but his friends were getting impatient. They had to head back home so the conversation was cut short."

Brad was waiting for me after work, I forgot that I said I would go over to his house. When we got there his parents wanted to take us out for dinner. I didn't want Brad to know that I really didn't want to go, I just smiled and said, "Sure".

We went to a restaurant called The Season Tavern, everything was going well. Although the atmosphere was nice I got caught up watching the different types of people who came through the door. I noticed someone in a baseball uniform, that seemed out of place. This restaurant certainly wasn't for a person in a baseball uniform. The uniform looked a bit familiar. Brad's mother was asking me a question but I didn't hear anything she said. Once I get my mind set on something there's no stopping me. I was looking right over the top of Brad's mother's head trying to see if it really was Johnny. That was definitely his uniform. It would have made things easier if it wasn't, I could just go on with dinner and try to get Johnny out of my mind. There was a rather attractive young woman standing right in front of his face and I still wasn't sure it was him. Then she stepped aside, it was him! My heart began to pound faster. It was Johnny, and he was with another woman. I wanted to jump from the table, wrap my hands around his neck and drag him out of the restaurant. Maybe even punch him as hard as I could and knock him out. I know I had no right to feel the way I was feeling. I was no longer in control of my mind. We weren't dating, we weren't together. I still couldn't help feeling the way I did. It was like being in prison locked up behind solid bars. I couldn't even compete with this woman because I was stuck with someone else. What was I suppose to do get up in front of my boyfriend's family? What could I say to excuse myself? I have some business to take care of? I don't think it would have worked. I was trapped. Looking through a glass window to the other room, I could see where the hostess sat him. I watched my future crumble. My eyes were burning, my fists were locked I didn't know how much longer I could sit there.

"We should probably get going." Brad's mother said.

At that moment I felt a sense of relief. I didn't have to watch this on going love affair between Johnny and some mystery woman. I didn't want to face him again. I made up my mind I was never speaking to him. As I sat on Brad's porch trying to remain calm, Johnny came home. He immediately ran up to me. He was excited because he beat my brother's baseball team. I could understand his enthusiasm considering my bother's team is undefeated. I kept picturing Johnny with that other young woman. I really didn't care about his baseball game. He didn't even notice I was barely saying anything. He ran off yelling. It was then that the blue car with the black top picked him up. Driving the car was the young woman that I saw at The Season Tavern. Her long flowing red hair covered her hideous appearance. What did he see in her? I could feel my face rising to unbearable temperatures. I knew I had to do something but, I wasn't thinking straight.

I put my negative energy into a nasty letter. I couldn't sleep that night anyway. I figured I might as well do something constructive.

In the letter I wrote that I wanted him to forget I had sent the rose. I didn't want anything to do with him because he drinks too much. That wasn't really the truth. Maybe I should have written what I was really feeling instead of some excuse.

That young woman could have been a relative or a good friend. I mailed the letter the next morning. I didn't think about it too much because I was so angry.

The letter got to him sooner than I had planned. That day Johnny came into the record store. He pretended to be looking for a new cassette. A cassette I knew that he already had. He didn't say anything about the letter, but I could tell he got it. It wasn't until that very moment that I realized I wasn't being fair.

I wanted things to happen so fast I wasn't even giving him a chance. After work, I was really feeling down. My brother's baseball games always cheered me up so, that's where I headed. Maybe I went there because I had a feeling Johnny would be there and he was. I felt I could handle seeing him this time. He walked by me and said hello. He then went to talk to some friends who were standing near me. I didn't turn around but I could hear his voice.

I wanted so desperately to talk to him but I just walked away. I didn't look back. I went home and went to bed. This whole Johnny thing was wearing me out.

Johnny never seemed to be home anymore. I didn't know what to do. I was going away for the weekend with Brad. The only thing I could really do was send Johnny another letter apologizing for the last one. By the time I returned, he would have enough time to think. He had to get it as soon as possible.

I decided to deliver it in person. He got out of work at the same time everyday. I waited outside for him. He came running out and jumped in his car. I waved my arms and flagged him over. As I walked slowly to his car, he opened his door and got out. When he saw that I had a envelope in my hand, he stopped.

"No", he replied in a nasty manner, "Is this another one of your mean letters?"

"No" I said.

"My sister said you called and hung up on her."

"I did not hang up on her, I said I would call back later."

"What did you want anyway?" he asked in a soft tone.

"Actually I wanted to know if you wanted to go to the movies."

"Oh?" Johnny said with interest.

Johnny had me so nervous I almost forgot how to speak.

"I better get going, is that all you wanted?" Johnny asked.

I didn't know what to say. There were so many things I wanted to tell him.

I knew it wasn't the right time so I said nothing. I just watched him drive away in his black Mustang. I felt helpless. I walked away with my head hung low in disappointment. That was the only opportunity I had to talk to him before I left on my weekend trip. Why couldn't I talk to him and tell him how I really felt?

I was a nervous wreck. I'm surprised I managed to answer his questions. I should have mailed the letter instead of delivering it in person. That was such a bad idea. I didn't mean to hurt his feelings. I couldn't believe his sister said I hung up on her.

She didn't know I was Johnny's secret admirer. I didn't want her to find out, so I never left my name. I guess she calls that hanging up. It wasn't like I didn't say good-bye. She obviously thought I was rude. She must have told him I hung up on her to get even.

My letter really hit home. However, not in a good way. I guess he didn't see the humor in it. Then again, neither did I. When I care about someone I don't think before I speak. It's a good excuse anyway. Maybe a defense I guess. When I hurt I want someone to hurt as bad as I do. I try not to be that way but, I can't seem to control it.

I had to go on this trip with Brad's family for the weekend and I was leaving the next day. How could I go knowing that Johnny was upset? How could I possibly have a good time?

The whole time I was on the trip, I couldn't help but think about everything he said. I kept rolling it around in my mind over and over again. I just wanted to cry. I was still in shock, so I didn't. I could hear the letter repeating in my head.

Dear Johnny:

I wanted to apologize for the last letter I wrote. I only said those things because I knew you weren't interested in me. I wanted to know if there could ever be anything between us? I like someone else on my brother's baseball team anyway. If you could just let me know somehow, I could get on with my life.

Pam

The letter wasn't exactly true. Actually it wasn't true at all. That's when I knew everything was going to come to an end. If there was anything there, it wasn't there anymore. If I told him I liked someone else I thought he would have told me how he felt.

My brother Pete was on the phone with my mother when I returned home.

"How was Pam's trip?" Pete asked

"She said she had fun." Mom said.

"That's good. He went on, Johnny wrote Pam a letter, it's not good."

"What did it say?" Mom asked.

"He just wants to remain friends."

"That's too bad I thought he liked her."

"Is it really serious to Pam?" Pete asked.

"Yes, it's serious."

My mom told me everything Pete said. I was too upset to read the letter when I got to work. Until curiosity got to me and I couldn't wait another second.

Dear Pam:

I think it would be better if we remain friends. I don't feel it's right.

Johnny

It was the worst day of my life. I had a sick feeling in my stomach. I felt like there was a knife through my chest. I kept telling everyone I was all right but, they knew I wasn't.

That night my brother called me to ask if I wanted to get an ice cream at Friendly's.

I said, "Sure."

Ice cream is always the solution to problems my brother and I have. It always makes us feel better. As we were sitting there eating hot fudge sundaes, Pete came out with the big question.

"What's up with you and Johnny Salve?" Pete asked.

"I've liked him for awhile I just never said anything before."

"You know Pam, it's hard because your boyfriend and he are neighbors and they are friends. With my friends, we would never date each others girlfriends."

"I guess you're right, but when I was younger it didn't matter who you went out with. Nobody cared, we never stayed with the same person."

"That isn't how it is now. You have to give him time. He doesn't know if you're going to run back to your old boyfriend. Wait a year, then see what happens."

"I thought if you really cared about someone it didn't matter who they dated before."

"Life isn't that simple." Pete replied.

"I know that now."

"Give it time."

I felt a lot better talking to my brother. He always makes me feel better. He gave me hope that one day maybe Johnny will come around. I was all ready to wait as long as it took.

CHAPTER 2

A few days went by. I hadn't seen Johnny since he yelled at me in the parking lot at work. Maybe he calmed down since then. I hoped he isn't the type to hold grudges for a long time. It's possible that there's a chance that he'll see me and forget I ever wrote that letter. I had to find away to see him, which wasn't very hard to do since his sister is my best friend.

Johnny's sister Kate and Diana were outside sitting on the porch. They were soaking up the fresh air with Diana's new born baby girl Mary. Her baby was adorable with dark hair and brown eyes. She was wearing a pretty pink dress with a white bonnet and little white shoes. She looked so cute.

"It looks like it's time for my little angel to eat her lunch." said Diana.

"Why don't you girls come in. We can talk some more while Diana feeds the baby." Kate suggested.

"Sure I would love to come in." I replied.

Of course I was going to say yes! This was the perfect way to get in the house to see Johnny. If I could only manage to stay in the house long enough for Johnny to come home from work. I was very patient and calm while waiting for Johnny to walk through that door. Every car that went by sounded like his. I must have been looking at the clock every minute. Praying he was going to come straight home from work. Then I heard the noise of feet stomping up the stairs. I sat up straight and tried to remain calm. The door opened and he was surprised to see me sitting there especially at his dining room table. You could tell by his facial expression. I couldn't tell if he forgave me for the letter. But, for that minute everything felt just fine. He walked over and kissed the baby on the cheek. My mind wandered. I was thinking about him coming home to our children.

He was really busy that dayand didn't talk much. He got on the phone with his friend. It really didn't matter to me because I got a chance to be with him no matter what he was doing. He was in such a hurry, he rushed out the door. I was hoping he was going to sit and talk with us but, it didn't happen. Diana started talking about their class reunion and how her and Johnny were going to see old friends.

It came time to leave Johnny's house. Believe me I didn't want to go. Samantha and Jane were getting tired of sitting there.

"I think it's time for us to be going home." Samantha said.

"Yes, we probably should go, it's getting late." Jane answered.

"I guess I'm going with them." I replied.

"See you later." Diana said.

Jane and I were outside on the porch waiting for Johnny to come home. I don't know what she was waiting for. We started talking about her love life, it was always so interesting. She always had a boyfriend.

As we were laughing, which is something Jane could always make me do Johnny pulled up in his jet black Mustang. He didn't see us on the porch. When he came back out, I wanted to say something to catch his attention.

"Hey ugly." I yelled.

Of all the things I had to say, it just slipped out. I couldn't say, "Hey Johnny." No, I had to insult him by accident. I couldn't take it back.

"I don't think he heard you." Jane yelled.

Johnny turned around and looked.

I said it again, "I said Hi ugly."

Johnny just smirked with anger and drove away.

"He's so cute! I would go out with him any day." Jane said.

I didn't say anything. I didn't want her thinking that I had feelings for him. Maybe she already knew. She may have detected something when he walked through the door. My hands shook, my face turned red and I became quiet. I was afraid to talk in his presence. The signs were all there. I knew I had to say something for if I didn't answer she would know.

"He's all right I guess." I answered.

"You have bad taste! Oh, that's right I forgot you date my brother." She chuckled.

I really wasn't into this conversation. I could only think about Johnny he still wasn't talking to me. I thought he would have forgiven me by now. There's nothing I can do to take back what I said. He might never talk to me again.

He'll get over it I hope. I know apologizing doesn't make how you feel go away. I should have never said something I didn't mean. I could have blown my whole plan.

CHAPTER 3

It was Friday and tonight was the night of Johnny's class reunion. I knew Johnny wasn't going to be around I decided to go to my house and take a break from all the commotion. It was my only day of rest. I had to try and clear my head. It was my family cookout tomorrow and I wanted to have a good time with my relatives. It was my day to forget about Johnny.

It was great having all this time to myself to think things over. It was time to reload my brain, to try to get back on track. At times I wished I never started this. That I could close my eyes and it would all go away. I knew it wasn't going to be that easy. It didn't seem fair giving up the only thing I cared for. I asked myself over and over what attracts me to this man, this beast?

I came up with nothing. I had no reason for loving this man. Maybe it was love at first sight. I've heard people say that it has happened. It's very difficult for me to believe that could happen but they say the chemistry was there. I know the way I felt. I wasn't happy with my life. I was always looking for something else. When Johnny came into my life I felt that was the solution to my problems. The chance to start over. Are my feelings real or is my mind playing tricks on me? All I know is he's the one I want to see everyday. The man to share my secrets and my dreams. How can I find a man that I can never hold or kiss? I will never know his soft lips and his strong gripping arms. It only angers me that I can never feel his touch.

I know Johnny wouldn't understand why I hadn't left Brad if I care about him so much. It's only because I'm scared of being alone. Taking the chance that Johnny might not ever want to be with me. There was too much at stake. If I can't have Johnny I'll live a miserable life with Brad. It's not worth loosing both men and I'm not ready to leave Brad behind.

I want more than this small town. Something always seemed to be missing. To me, Johnny is the perfect man. Maybe that's what I'm missing. Brad just doesn't seem to be perfect. Johnny could be my solution to true happiness. What if I date Johnny and it's all wrong? Am I going to leave or will I be afraid to hurt his feeling's too? Anyone would seem perfect to me. Brad is always putting me down, saying I can't do certain things. He never wants me to achieve. He picks on me for the smallest thing. The other day we were going out to lunch at a sub shop that we often eat at. Before we entered the door he said, "You always order the same sub why don't you try something different?"

"I really don't like anything else," I replied.

"How do you know if you don't try?" he said.

"I see, I'm suppose to order a sub that I don't like, don't eat it, and pay for it."

"You're so boring. I'm always trying new things." Brad said.

"I didn't know I wasn't allowed to eat what I wanted. You have gotten many subs you didn't like and threw away. Later you're starving."

"That's my choice."

"Right and this is my choice. I'll eat what I want."

It was all incredibly ridiculous that he wanted to start controlling my every decision. We were at a bad point in our relationship. We were always fighting about something stupid. We couldn't do anything without fighting. I tried talking to him but, it didn't work. He only said, "This is who I am and if you don't like it, I don't really care." How could such a good relationship go bad? I always thought Brad was the one. Now seeing this other side of him not caring for my feelings, it hurts. There were days I didn't want to get out of bed. I knew Brad would be calling for me to go down his house.

This one day everything went wrong. Brad called to see what I was doing.

"Where were you, it's twelve?" Brad asked.

"I was sleeping."

"Why don't you get dressed and get down here."

"I was going to go out with my mother shopping." I said.

"Well, I'm not going shopping so you can come over when you're done."

"That's fine." I replied.

"What time are you going to be back?" Brad asked.

"I have no idea."

"Fine I'll see you when you get back." he said.

My mom and I had a wonderful day. When I got to Brad he had an angry look on his face.

"Where did you go?" he said.

“I went shopping and out to lunch.”

“You went out to lunch? What about me? I’ve been sitting here waiting.” he said.

“We went over to the mall and there was a restaurant we wanted to try.” I defended.

“You should have come back and got me.” he said.

“I’m suppose to leave the mall to pick you up when I’m already there?”

“Yes, I’m starving.”

“Next time eat. You told me you didn’t want to come. All you did was sit in the house? It was time for me to get a break from you and this house.” I shouted.

“You could have picked me up.”

“Last week when my mother and I went shopping we stopped by to pick you up for lunch and you said no.”

“This time was different.”

“Why? You never want to go! You're only doing this to start a fight.”

“Why don’t you go home.” Brad shouted.

I walked out. I didn’t need to listen to this anymore and I’m tired of feeling this empty pit in my stomach. I need to have someone that picks me up and makes me feel like a person again. I know Johnny is that person. He’s the one that can fill this void. I often wonder if Johnny feels the same way. Does he want to date me and he’s scared of me? Or, maybe he's afraid of what Brad will say. How much longer must I hide these feelings for him? I won't feel any loss if he never comes around. Although he was the one who taught me what love really was.

CHAPTER 4

It turned out to be a wonderful day. Outside the sun was beaming warming the ground around us. It was a perfect day for a family cook out.

My relatives gathered in the back yard. They were having the time of their lives soaking up the sun, eating hamburgers and hot dogs. My grandmother was in the corner sipping tea and laughing at the kids playing jump rope. My uncles were sitting in the lawn chairs reminiscing old times back when they were children. The day couldn't have been better. This was what life was all about good memories, things you never seem to forget. That one thing when you look back and remember, always seems to make you smile. It was a good time to catch up on old times.

My brother Charlie and my sister-in-law Karen walked in about a half hour late, as usual. They were wearing sunglasses of course, to cover up the vicious hang over from the night before.

Anything for a party. At all of the family cook outs we have, they're wearing sunglasses. They're always trying to cover up some mishap. I'm sure they had a wonderful time at the reunion. I could see them now, dancing and drinking.

"Mom, Johnny Salve was beat up last night. We saw him on crutches" my brother Charlie said.

"You're kidding, what happened?"I asked. They were in such a daze that they never heard what I said. They kept rambling on and on. The two of them sounded like little kids fighting over who was going to tell the story. I repeated myself again!

"What happened?" I said.

"We don't know. All we heard was that he was with one of his friends and some people started with him."

At that point you might as well have punched me out. It was hard for me ,not knowing if he was all right. What a day! What a day for him, how could something so bad happen? I couldn't get my mind off whether he was all right or not. What bothered me most was that I couldn't get near him to help. We weren't talking to each other. The only thing I could do was sit by and watch. It was like telling a pro football player to sit on the side lines and watch everyone else play. I knew if I saw him, I could look into his eyes. I would know if he was all right. The only problem was, I was here and I didn't know where he was. I felt trapped. I wished I could hold him and tell him everything would get better, but I couldn't.

As I looked around at my relatives, I realized their life seemed settled. They accomplished their goals. They're all married with children and they seem happy with their simple lives. I want more than this. I want to be sitting here with Johnny Salve married with kids and reminisce with my brothers. I want to achieve all my goals like they did. I know these things take time. But I haven't fulfilled my dreams. Isn't that what life is about to achieve certain dreams and accomplish what we want to do? Life is one big challenge, a maze and you have to pick the right way to go. Someday I will have what my relatives have.

Each day after Johnny's accident, I wondered why I was making a mistake like this. Why am I holding on to a boyfriend I don't love? What could possibly be holding me back? Then it all became clear. If I left Brad, I wouldn't be able to see Johnny anymore. It was a tough decision to make. I was in love with my boyfriends next door neighbor. I wasn't getting anywhere by staying in the relationship. It meant giving up my right to see Johnny. My last decision was to wait it out until Johnny got better. Then it was time for me to go.

There were many unsaid things. Would I really like being with Johnny? Did I love Brad? If I dated Johnny would I want to be with Brad? Was I going to regret this? Could this be the biggest mistake of my life? These questions kept coming up over and over. Why was this such a big decision? I know I have feelings for Johnny. When did it become so hard? If I date Johnny will he fulfill my needs? Will I make this decision then change my mind and go back to Brad? I can't do that to Johnny. It was like a crow cawing he only makes one sound. Is that my life, getting into a relationship and then wanting to date someone else? Was it going to be like monopoly where the game never ends? I was scared. I didn't want to make the wrong move. Is Johnny going to forget about me if I leave Brad? Will he ask me out? I was confused. I didn't have a clue what to do. My feelings were bouncing up and down like a super ball. I really don't know Johnny very well. What if he has a dark side that no one knows about. I know his family, but I don't know him. Maybe I should stay with Brad for a couple more months and get to know Johnny a little better. Then he might think I'm staying with Brad and I could risk losing him forever. What if he finds someone else, he could forget me. I would never be able to forgive myself. I really didn't have much of a choice. I had to leave Brad and except the consequences. If I didn't move in now, I would lose my dream man forever. I wanted to ask someone for advice but, I already knew what they would say:

"Oh, you have been with Brad for such a long time you can't throw all those years away. You have to stick it out. I promise you it will get better, you'll see."

No! I'm not going to lose Johnny over someones opinion. They don't know how miserable I am inside. They can't feel my pain. I was putting all my effort into Johnny. I was going to win him over like a horse in the Kentucky Derby. He was going to be mine forever. I'm not giving up on him. I'm taking charge of my life. Like a boulder crashing down into the quarries, he isn't going to know what hit him.

CHAPTER 5

It was an ordinary day in June. My mother was on her way to get new tires for her Ford Bronco. I had nothing else to do so I went along for the ride. We were baby-sitting that day. It must have been some kind of holiday because they were off from school. My niece and nephew Matt and Emily, what a couple of clowns. They always made you laugh.

Sitting there in the Ford Bronco Matt started to talk about Johnny Salve. I don't know why, but he just blurted it out. Me being nosy, I thought I would try to get some more information out of Matt.

"Since we're on the subject how do you two like Johnny?" I asked.

"I'm going to marry him." Matt laughed.

Matt was always making jokes about something. He was never serious about anything. He was only a kid and he sure was funny.

"Yeah, I like him. I think he's funny, not as funny as Matt, but funny." Emily replied.

I felt a lot better that Emily and Matt liked Johnny. My niece and nephew were a big part of my life and if anybody had to like Johnny it was them.

After we had the tires changed, I decided to take my niece and nephew to Brad's house.

I was trying to spend as little time as I could with Brad I was spending a lot more time with my mother. Brad didn't seem to understand how close we are. It's probably because he is not close to his mother at all! Don't get me wrong I didn't want this relationship to end. I figured that maybe if we spent sometime away from each other, we would want to be with each other again. Maybe my problem of having feelings for someone else would end.

When I arrived at Brad's house Brad and his sisters were sitting at the kitchen table. That's where they usually sat.

"Hello everyone." I said.

"Hello." Jane said.

Jane was the friendlier of the two, she was always so full of life and excitement.

"Where did you go today?" Jane asked.

"Nowhere special, just to change my mother's tires at the shop."

"Oh how exciting."

"You're telling me." I replied.

"Brad I forgot to tell you Johnny Salve got a rose from someone!"

I thought I was going to hit the floor! I had to think of something to say fast before my face turned three different shades of pink. I tried not to be suspicious.

"Yeah! He has some secret admirer, can you believe that? Who would ever be interested in him? He doesn't know if he's coming or going."

Nice cover up! I should have never said the word secret admirer. Maybe they will never read the card.

Then again that's what everyone calls it when you get a letter with no name on it. I guess I'm safe for now. I'm glad that's over hopefully they'll forget all about it. I doubt it.

All Matt and Emily could think about was how they wanted to go swimming in Brad's pool.

"Brad, may we go swimming?" they both asked.

They decided to ask together because Matt was too shy to ask for himself.

"Sure I'll race you." Brad replied.

"Pam, are you going swimming?" Jane asked.

"No, I have to be heading off to work soon." I replied.

"How about if we just sit outside on the deck and talk?" Jane said.

"That sounds great!" I said.

"I'll race you." Jane laughed.

Jane beat me in the race of course. I was not in very good shape. I had to sit down and rest before I passed out. Jane and I didn't talk about much. We talked every day and she had no new stories for me. Jane loved to talk but she wasn't talking much today. Brad was trying to pull me in. I pulled back and gave Brad a dirty look and he stopped. I was completely sick of Brad's childish games. He may have been eighteen but ,he acted twelve. I was getting tired of sitting there. It was time to go to work. As much as I hated working I didn't mind going today. Now to try to get the kids to go home. That was a task in itself.

"Matt and Emily, I think it's time for us to go home." I said.

"Do we have to go? Can't we stay a little longer?" Emily asked.

"If you can reverse time we can stay." I replied.

"All right we can stay!" Emily cried.

"I was only kidding." I said.

"Oh figures, I knew it was too good to be true." Matt said.

"You guys really crack me up." I laughed.

By the time they got out of the pool and ready, I was already late. I was rushing the kids in the car. You know who was not ready, Brad. He was in the house getting changed. Like a girl slow and never ready. I guess no one cared if I was late for work. In all the commotion I was over looking one thing. I felt this little nudge from the back seat. It was Matt, he was pointing.

"Look Auntie Pam it's Johnny."

I slowly turned my head over to Johnny's house. There he was, Johnny Salve. His big smile looking right at me my heart dropped down to my stomach. My hands started to quiver.

"How are you feeling?" I asked.

He did not reply. I assumed he didn't hear me. All of a sudden I heard Emily and Matt laughing. They were laughing at what Matt said about Johnny.

"What are you laughing at?" Johnny asked.

"Matt was talking about you today and he said he wants to marry you." I replied.

We all chuckled except Matt who was still laughing from before.

"The kids really like you Johnny, they think you're funny." I said.

Just as we started to get into a conversation Brad came. Of all the times Brad has to show up. We said good bye and I drove off. We waved to each other and that was it. I didn't know when I would see him again.

"Auntie Pam."

"Yes Emily."

"I'm sorry but I left my shoes at the house."

Yes! It couldn't be any better timing than that my chance to see Johnny again. When we got back Johnny was already inside. I was extremely disappointed. I couldn't help but think of Johnny the whole time I was in work. With his strong hands and his crystal blue eyes he was everything I wanted in a man. He was also a man I was not supposed to have feelings for.

CHAPTER 6

I noticed things started to change. I was becoming more depressed. My days in bed were becoming longer. I didn't have much to get up to. Having to get up to be with a boyfriend I did not like being with was the hardest thing I have ever done. I didn't know how to tell him I was leaving him. I didn't want to hurt his feelings. I was angry with myself for getting involved with Brad but, how was I supposed to know it would be like this. Our relationship started off great. We spent every day together, that was when we enjoyed each others company. Then, Brad was attractive but something strange happened. Everyday I looked at Brad he became less and less attractive. Was it because I wasn't interested any more or was he really becoming unattractive? Many girls liked Brad then. He was always a lot of fun to be with. I also noticed he was really young for his age. I think that's why everybody liked him so much. That was one quality I did not find impressive. We had many good times together. Things changed and we no longer were happy with each other or our selves. I think we were both pretty depressed. We were always snapping at each other. Some days I wanted to choke him. At times he could be really mean and I could be too. All I kept thinking about was that I have to spend the rest of my life with this person. It just kept playing in my head over and over again like a truck driver's horn. We all know life can be short. There is no time to waste being with someone negative. Everything I wanted to do he would put me down. He would say I couldn't do that. I have a young mind with a lot of adventure to pursue, is that a crime? I must admit I was in love with him at one time, but things just went stale. Often at times I tried to find the love we once had but, it didn't seem to work out as planned. We would always end up fighting. That's when I got fed up I called it quits. I was at work, I don't know what came over me I was cracking up. I let him have it.

"Brad I can't take it any more. I mean, I try to make you happy but, I can't." I said.

It was surprising, Brad didn't say a word he only looked. The car ride was quiet. When I dropped him off he just got out of the car without saying anything. This was it! I finally had my freedom! I could cover new ground, see things I wanted to see and do things I wanted to do. Why do I feel this empty? Like I lost my best friend. I guess I really did lose my best friend. We gave up all of our friends when we started dating. He was the only friend I really had. At this point I didn't know how to feel. All I know was I felt really bad inside. I did not know I would feel this attached to one person, who knew. I would miss him, even the fights we had. I still have feelings for him but, there was no turning back now the damage was done. It was time for me to hit the road for more adventure and action.

CHAPTER 7

It wasn't long before I was back on my feet again. I was pursuing Johnny. Putting all my effort to win his heart over. I didn't send anymore roses but, there were a lot of letters. There was this one time when I decided to try something different . To try to get his attention. He was coming to my work a lot. I figured this was my best opportunity to make my move. I recorded a tape of three songs I was trying to capture my feelings. I tried to find songs that best described how I felt. Possibly something that might of happened that we had in common. It wasn't easy finding the songs and I didn't want to put one song on the tape. I wanted to go to the extreme and put three. They were all slow songs of course, the romantic ones always are. They described us pretty well. There were somethings we never did, but those were the best I could come up with. The last song always brought tears to my eyes. He was very special to me. It was hard to sit around and wait for a maybe I'll ask you out someday. I wanted to be with him. Was that hard to understand? Did he understand I never felt this way about anyone before? From the instant I saw him I knew he was the one. All these feelings all bundled up inside of me like a bag of groceries not put away. I wanted to march over his house like a soldier and demand him to take me out. I couldn't be any more pushy. I knew that wouldn't have worked out very well. He probably would have said excuse me, who do you think you are? I will ask you when I am good and ready if I even do ask. Now I don't know if I will. It's bad enough my nasty letter offended him. I didn't need to do anymore damage. I've caused enough trouble.

I really worked hard on that tape. I taped it over and over again until I got it right. It was a difficult job since I was having trouble with the recorder. However, I did manage. I must have changed my mind thirty different times. Should I send him the tape? Was I being too pushy? I thought maybe I should wait until he made the first move. I quickly changed my mind. I figured if he knows how much I care then he'll ask me out.

I was on edge today. I was rundown and irritated. I didn't feel like working. I wanted to call in sick, but I needed the money. I had to drag myself in. I'm glad I showed up it ended up to be the best day of my life, Johnny walked in.

"Pam I think we need to talk." Johnny said.

I didn't know what to say. I couldn't believe he was at my work, standing at the door telling me we have to talk. I tried to not look anxious.

"What do you want to talk about Johnny?" I asked.

"I think you know." Johnny said.

Johnny pulled out the tape I sent him from his jeans pocket. I almost died right there. Well, at least I know he got it. Now what was I suppose to say, "It wasn't from me?" I don't think he would have fell for that one.

"Meet me here after you get off work and we will talk about this. I'll be waiting." Johnny said.

Waving the tape in the air Johnny walked out the door. I was in a panic. What was he going to say to me? What was he going to do, beat me up and leave me on the side of the road because of a tape? The night dragged by I thought it would never end. I only had a certain amount of time to think about what I was going to say. I had to try to get out of this one. I surely didn't want him mad at me. I know what I will tell him, I lost my head. I had a weak moment. I was distracted with other things. Yeah, that's it. I'm sure I can come up with some excuse by 8:00 pm. I paced a lot and my time grew shorter. I still didn't have a plausible excuse. I was scared and shaking. I knew I had to try to calm down some how. I sat down and tried to relax a little, but nothing seemed to work. It was hopeless.

Eight o'clock time to close but, there was no sign of Johnny. Where could he be? He's probably not going to meet me after all. I tried to go about my business and lock up,trying to take my mind off Johnny. I tried telling myself it didn't really matter if he did show up. I don't care anymore, he doesn't know what he's missing. I waited patiently by the door looking at the big empty parking lot. There was no sign of Johnny.

At 8:20 I decided to go home. I figured he must have got caught up with some of his friends. As I walked away I took one more glance back, he still was not anywhere in sight.

"Where do you think you're going? I thought I told you to wait for me?" Johnny said.

"I didn't think you were going to show up." I smiled.

"When I say I'm going to be somewhere I'll be there." Johnny said in a stern voice.

" I didn't mean to offend you." I said.

"Don't worry about it." Johnny said.

Johnny walked towards me, he looked better than ever. He wore faded blue jeans, with a black tee shirt rolled up at the sleeves. A black baseball hat and black high top sneakers, he was incredible. He moved closer and closer until he was right in front of me.

"Now about this tape." Johnny said.

Before I could answer, Johnny put his finger over my mouth. I guess he didn't want to ruin the moment. Either that or he didn't want to hear my sad excuse.

"I had no idea you felt this way." Johnny said.

"I had no idea we would ever stand this close." I said.

Johnny laughed he must find me amusing. Who knew my tape would work so well. I should have made the tape sooner.

"How long have you felt this way?" Johnny asked.

"Since the first day I met you." I said quietly.

"You're kidding." Johnny said.

"No, I'm not kidding."

Johnny moved in closer and put his hands on my hips. He started acting a little weird, almost like he was happy. I felt strong next to him. Well my feelings were strong anyway.

"Johnny, I feel really bad about Brad. We were friends too." I sighed.

"Pam you shouldn't be sad. You and Brad breaking up is terrific, now we can be together." Johnny said.

"You don't think it's wrong? You are his next door neighbor. He's going to find out." I said.

Johnny grabbed my arms and shook me to try to get me to stop.

"Pam listen to me we will just sneak around he'll never know, I promise." Johnny said.

Johnny held me in his arms. He had this way of making you feel like everything was going to be all right. He instantly became a part of you.

"Are you going to be all right Pam?"

"Yes I feel a lot better now." I said.

"Are you cold? You're shaking" Johnny asked.

"Yes I am a little cold." I replied.

"You wait right here I know I have a jacket in my car." Johnny said.

It was the coolest jean jacket I ever saw it was a royal blue color. I never saw a jacket as nice as his. He wrapped the jacket around my arms.

"Thanks Johnny, what if you get cold?"

"Don't worry about me you're more important right now." Johnny replied.

I finally had the man of my dreams but, I was scared of the world. I didn't want anyone to be hurt. I didn't want Brad thinking that's why our relationship failed. If there was only another way around this mess. There wasn't if I wanted to keep Johnny. I had to listen to what he said, good or bad. He was what I wanted and I had to try and keep him. I didn't want him feeling like I still had feelings for Brad. I knew I would lose him for sure. He wasn't the type of guy who took things lightly. I had to show him I was only interested in him. I had to stop talking about Brad if I wanted

Johnny to stay. I did want Johnny to see my feelings for Brad were gone. Johnny's here now and he took all my feelings for Brad away. Brad was in the past, a lost time in Egypt, a treasure buried under sea. Yes, my feelings were gone forever. It's easier said than done. I'll try to talk my feelings for Brad away maybe I will convince myself they're gone.

CHAPTER 8

Johnny is coming over with some big surprise. He refuses to tell me what it is. I'm sure it's going to be very interesting. He told me to be ready in an hour, I said no problem. Whatever Johnny says I think I can manage to do it.

"Hey, Pam are we ready or what?" Johnny asked.

"We are ready Johnny, where are you taking me?" I asked.

"Pam you know I'm not going to tell you that."

"I was just checking." I joked.

Johnny smiled. "You didn't think it was going to be that easy?"

"I didn't think so."

Johnny ran to open the door for me. "Here you go my lady." Johnny smiled.

"Oh thank you darling." I chuckled.

"So where are we going?"

"Nice try again Pam." Johnny smirked.

We were hitting it off! It was as if I knew him for a long time. We were driving for sometime but, it somehow didn't seem that long with Johnny.

"This is it! What do you think?" Johnny asked.

"It's beautiful, I love it it's the best place in the world." I replied.

Johnny brought me to this great big parking lot with a cement wall. Behind it was the sparkling ocean, great big waves crashed along the ocean wall, it was magnificent. Johnny couldn't help but look into my eyes the way the waves reflected off them. The way my face moved every time a wave crashed along the wall it was beautiful. He was glad he took me here and that I liked it so much.

"Pam, come on."

Johnny grabbed my hand and he started running. It looked as if we were flying like sea gulls. It looked like we would be together forever.

"Pam hold on."

Johnny and I leaped over the wall. With a single bound we dropped down into the water. What a splash, the water rose up our bodies in full force. We ran along the seashore splashing and jumping like two little kids at a playground.

"Johnny this is wonderful, thank you very much."

"Pam I wanted to show you a good time because, I know Brad never did."

I got quiet, I didn't want to remember Brad. I was trying to forget him.

"What's wrong Pam, did I say something wrong?" Johnny asked.

"Yeah, you mentioned Brad."

"You're kidding right? I can't even mention his name, that's unbelievable."

"Johnny what's the problem, would you calm down?"

"Don't tell me to calm down."

Johnny started walking in front of me, I grabbed his arm. "Johnny wait! You have to understand something. My feelings can't just go away for Brad that easy it's going to take time." I said.

"Pam how long is it going to take, I thought we were doing great together."

I grabbed both Johnny's arms and brought him toward me. I rested his head on my shoulder.

"Pam I don't want to lose you." Johnny cried.

"I know." Johnny and I embraced for along time hoping we could resolve this problem. Hoping to stay together without hurting each other. I knew it was going to take some time before Johnny would trust me not to go back to Brad. Why would I want to give up Johnny? He was always a pleasure to be around. I liked spending time with him. Unlike Brad who wanted to sit in the house all day long and watch TV. This was not my idea of fun. Johnny was special, if only I could express myself so that he would feel safe with this relationship. He didn't want to lose me and I didn't want to lose him. That was definitely worth trying for.

"Johnny, why don't we sit for a while?" I took Johnny's hand to sit down as he walked with his head down in distress. We sat on the soft sand and watched the sea gulls fly into the clouds.

"Sometimes I wish I could take off like those birds." Johnny said.

I squeezed Johnny's hand tighter. "I wish we could fly up there, with the wind catching our wings. We would glide through the sunset without a care in the world." I said.

Johnny layed back, stretched out his elbow so I could rest my head. He didn't want me to get sand in my hair.

"Pam why don't you rest for a while, if we stay tonight we could see the stars."

Johnny and I had such a rough day that we grew tired fast. We cuddled up next to each other to stay warm, it was nice. Johnny awoke in the night to watch the stars. He never looked at the stars at all, he watched me sleep for hours. I felt so peaceful and Johnny couldn't help but stare. He stroked my hair gently and touched my smooth silky skin. Johnny couldn't believe I stayed with him the whole night. I bet he wondered what I saw in him. He asked me when I woke up.

"What time is it, Johnny?"

"It's just in time to watch the sunrise."

"Oh good, I thought I was going to miss it." Johnny and I watched the sunrise. The sun was bright red with a touch of orange. It was a beautiful sight. There I was at the ocean with the man of my dreams. Embraced in his arms like a bear skin rug. When I looked up at him he would give me a smile that lit up the sky. You could tell he felt it too by the way he looked at me. As he looked into my eyes you could tell he only saw me. If the world collapsed around me he wouldn't even notice. He only saw me and nothing else. He really knew how to make me feel special.

"Pam, isn't this wonderful I wish we could stay here forever." Johnny said.

"Johnny, I know it's hard but we're going to make it we just have to stick together." I convinced him.

"Pam are you sure we can't stay here forever." Johnny smiled.

"Yes, I'm sure. We can always come back here

to visit."

"Every day?" Johnny asked.

"Not every day we both have to work." I said.

"Someday you and I are going to live in a great big house along the shore. The waves will crash against our house while we watch the sunrise every morning. To watch the sea gulls fly through the sky, wouldn't it be wonderful, Pam?"

"Someday Johnny, someday."

Johnny lifted me up and swung me around like a carousel.

"What do you think, I'm kidding?"

"Oh, I'm sorry I thought you were lying." I chuckled.

"You think that's funny." Johnny joked. Johnny tickled me till I couldn't breathe.

"OK! I quit." I smiled.

"You're lucky." Johnny laughed.

"Oh really, you only gave up because you thought I couldn't breathe, well I fooled you." I laughed.

"That's it, I'm going to get revenge." Johnny laughed. Johnny continued to tickle me.

"OK I take it back, you win."

"I thought you would see it my way." Johnny laughed.

"Come on Johnny I'll race you."

Johnny and I ran so fast we thought we would just drop right there. Neither of us wanted the other to win.

"How about we call it quits." Johnny said.

"OK, you first it was your idea." I smiled.

"Oh, I know then you will say you won." Johnny said.

"You're right! That was what I had planned." I

laughed.

"All right but I want a re-match."

"You got it." I shouted.

Johnny and I dropped to the sand like boulders at the quarries, we were exhausted.

There's nothing like a morning run to break in the day." Johnny smiled.

"You can say that again." I agreed.

"There's nothing like a morning run to break in the day." Johnny repeated.

"I didn't mean for you to repeat it." I laughed.

"I knew that I was just kidding around."

"Yeah, I'm sure you were, you thought I was serious." I laughed.

"Pam, I see a place to eat you stay here I'll run over and get you something." Johnny said.

"OK, Johnny I'll just sit here along the shore." I said.

"Is there something special that you would like?" he asked.

"No, anything you get will be just fine." I said.

"I'll be right back. Don't you go anywhere." Johnny hinted.

"I'm only going to take a couple of laps around the ocean. It might take a couple days but, hopefully I'll be back before breakfast." I smirked.

"Oh, very funny." Johnny said.

"See you in a little bit."

I wanted to reassure Johnny I wasn't going anywhere. I liked being with him he was very thoughtful and kind. Johnny leaned over and kissed me on the cheek.

"I'll be right back."

This was the perfect time to kick back and watch

the waves splashing against the surface. How the cool sand refreshed your body and the sun's rays beats upon my face. I watched the sea gulls swoop down into the water and bring out a great big fish. It was things people only dreamed about. Johnny was right, I wish we never had to leave here, everything was perfect. Gigantic mansions covered the shore line, maybe one day Johnny and I will live here.

Crash! Oh my, what was that ! I turned my head to see what happened. There was a car in the middle of the road. Maybe the car hit one of the sea walls. That's probably what happened. It must be serious, I can hear the ambulance siren. I was afraid to look. I was scared it was going to be Johnny. I knew I had no choice but to look.

I walked up toward the sea wall very slowly. I didn't want to see what might have happened. I looked over the sea wall and saw a person lying in the road. He was unconscious and very still. I quickly turned my head away. I knew I had to get a closer look. I was too far away to be able to tell if it was Johnny. I was shaking with every step I took. I kept thinking, what if it's Johnny. I hope it's not, I was frightened. As I came up on the body, I looked up and there was Johnny. He was standing at the coffee shop with two coffee rolls, two orange juices and plenty of napkins. What a relief! My stomach was in knots. I stood there a moment and froze it was so nice to see him again. I quickly ran back to where I was sitting when he left. I didn't want him to think I was going to be worried every time I heard an ambulance. I also didn't want him to think I left him after I promised I wasn't going anywhere. He would have been worried.

"Hey babe, did you miss me?"

Johnny sat behind me and gave me a hug and a kiss on the cheek.

"Did I ever." I replied.

"I got you a coffee roll I hope you like them, and an orange juice to drink."

"Sure, I love orange juice. I drink it every morning and I like coffee rolls too."

"Good. I'm glad you like them. I didn't know what to get you."

I leaned over and gave Johnny a piece of my coffee roll. "I want you to try it first in case it's poison or something." I laughed.

"Oh, sure kill me off first." Johnny replied.

"How's it taste?" I asked.

"It's good here try some."

Johnny shoved the coffee roll right into my face.

"You right it is good why don't you finish mine." I rubbed the coffee roll all over his face.

"How does it taste now?" I asked.

"Even better." Johnny laughed.

There, the two of us sat with coffee rolls smashed all over our faces. We looked really attractive.

"Well, so much for breakfast."

"It's not over yet." Johnny smiled. Johnny leaned over and gave me a kiss with his sticky face. He thought he was being funny. Let's see who has the last laugh.

"Johnny, why don't you wash that off?" I opened my orange juice and splashed him right in the face.

"That's it woman, this is revenge." Johnny picked me up over his head and walked me toward the ocean. I was in big trouble now. Johnny threw me into the water. His plan back fired when he fell in right after me. I couldn't stop laughing.

"Oh you think that's funny?" Johnny splashed water into my face.

"I happen to think it's really funny." I replied.

"Come over here let me give you a hug." Johnny coaxed.

"How do I know you're not planning something?" I smiled.

"Would I do that?" he said.

"Yes." I replied.

"You're the one that will be missing out."

"All right." I said. Well, Johnny really wasn't kidding he really did give me a hug. I knew I could trust him, he always did what he said. You could always count on Johnny. I knew I would never be disappointed with him. He would never tell you something and not do it.

"It's getting cold, do you want to get out?" Johnny asked.

"Yeah, we probably should be going home. I do have to work tonight." I replied.

Johnny and I walked the shore line one last time. Our toes sank into the wet sand. While the sea gull flew over head the waves still crashed the surface. It was everything I ever wanted and more. Johnny made all this possible, he was really something else.

CHAPTER 9

After all the excitement with Johnny, I had to have a night out with the girls. They always give me the best advice.

"Look at this lovely red dress it gives off a glow." I said.

"It's really sexy." Louise said.

"Oh, red is always sexy." Margo explained.

"What do you think?" I asked.

"Wait a minute, you only buy a dress when you're interested in someone." Louise commented. Louise was the smart one, blond with a body to die for. Smart and good looking.

"Who is it?" Margo asked. Margo was always getting the gossip. She knew everything that was going on. She never missed a trick.

"Johnny Salve." I replied.

"No way, you're kidding?" Sally asked. Sally never thought anything was possible. I don't think she believes anything you say. I don't even think she believes her mother is her own flesh and blood.

"What about Brad?" Louise asked.

"We started to drift apart." I explained.

"How did you meet this Johnny Salve?" Margo said.

"You know, Johnny Salve is Brad's neighbor we met through Brad." I explained.

"I can't believe it, I thought for sure you would be with Brad forever." Sally muttered.

"I thought we would too. When I first met Johnny I couldn't breathe. He was remarkably attractive." I gloated.

"Can we meet him?" Margo asked.

"Sure" I said.

"When?" Margo asked.

"Soon." I replied.

"How soon, tomorrow?" Sally asked.

"I can't believe you people are this impatient you really want to meet him tomorrow?" I said.

"Well, you've been telling us how gorgeous he is. You expect us to wait? I don't think so." Margo said.

"I guess you're right." I said.

"Don't listen to them they probably want to sink their paws on him." Louise said.

Margo and Sally looked down ashamed.

"You can't be serious I thought you were my friends. I'm not worried and Johnny would never be interested in you."

"Oh, you're sure of yourself." Sally said.

"I'm not going to fight over this." I snapped.

"You're right we're sorry for thinking something like that. We wouldn't have really tried taking him away from you. We only want to see how gorgeous he really is." Margo explained.

I hugged Margo. "Thanks for being my friends I couldn't have picked a better bunch." I smiled.

"Pam let's buy that red dress Johnny will love it on you! Margo exclaimed.

"You have the perfect figure." Louise said.

"You girls really know how to make me feel attractive, I only hope Johnny will like it." I smiled.

"Pam don't forget we have to get you some shoes. We don't want Johnny saying he's never going out with you again because you don't have matching shoes." Sally laughed.

"Where are you going?" Margo asked.

"He's taking me to this exquisite restaurant in Hingham." I gloated.

"Wow! I heard Hingham is a fancy town." Louise said.

"Does this Johnny, have any friends?" Margo asked.

"As a matter a fact he does, though I've never met him." I explained.

"Maybe we should go on a double date?" Margo asked.

"Get out of here Margo. You can find your own dates." I laughed.

"I forgot, now we're Miss fancy." Margo chuckled.

"These shoes couldn't be any more perfect!" Sally exclaimed. The shoes were red with three diamonds. They sparkled when the light hit them just right.

"These shoes are beautiful. Thanks Sally for finding them you always have a good eye for fashion." I praised.

"Well, girls I think I'm ready for my extraordinary date." I chuckled.

"You ought to hurry up it's getting late and you

don't want to miss your date." Louise suggested.

"You're right, I only have an hour I really lost track of time." I said.

"Let's go." Margo said.

"Thanks for your help." I smiled.

"Any time Pam." Louise said.

"I'll call you later to tell you how it went." I said.

"OK Pam, bye." Louise said.

I ran home from the store. I only had forty-five minutes left by the time I got home. I had to meet Johnny down on Main St. in front of the flower shop at seven. I threw on my clothes, my make up, and I was out the door by seven fifteen. It gave me just enough time to get to the flower shop. When I arrived, Johnny wasn't there yet. The time seemed to be going by so quickly. First it was seven, then it was seven thirty. I started to worry about Johnny. I hoped he was all right. At seven forty-five I knew he stood me up. I didn't know how to feel. My head lifted up from staring at the ground. Tears started to trickle down my face. I waited long enough, I wanted to go home, lay down on my bed and cry.

"Pam wait, don't go! Johnny yelled.

I turned around my sweet Johnny was running toward me. Johnny grabbed me and held me tight.

"I'm glad you're still here. I didn't want you mad at me." he apologized.

"Johnny what happened to you?" I asked.

"My car broke down up the street and I've been trying to fix it. I didn't want to ruin our date. I'm sorry Pam."

I placed my hand on Johnny's back. I wanted to make him feel secure. I hated to see him upset.

"Johnny, don't worry about it. You didn't ruin our date. It doesn't matter where you take me, I only want to be with you."

Johnny looked up at me in surprise. "Really?"

"Yes really."

Johnny took my hand, and we walked along the sidewalk looking at all the little shops.

"You wait right here, Pam." Johnny ran into a flower shop.

"Here Pam I think it's about time I gave you a rose." Johnny explained. The rose was incredible. It was wrapped in pretty red paper. A little card that said, *Thank you for not getting mad at me, Johnny*. I gave Johnny a hug and a kiss.

"I could never be mad at you." The minute you looked in Johnny's eye's you knew he could do no wrong. He had some sort of magic.

"Pam, would you like to get something to eat in here? I know it's not fancy, but it's food."

"Anything is fine with me."

"What would you like my lady in red?"

"I would like the pizza please. I heard it's exquisite." I chuckled.

"The young lady will have pizza please." Johnny said.

"You got it, young man." the chef replied.

This was more fun than any fancy restaurant. It was romantic and it added a certain zest to the evening.

"This place is great, Johnny!" I exclaimed.

"I use to come here when I was a kid with my father."

"It's wonderful." I said.

"I'm glad you like it. I was afraid you wouldn't."

"Why wouldn't I like this place?" I asked.

"I promised you that we would go to the fancy restaurant." he said.

"This place is more my style any way. You always have to worry when you're at fancy places." I said.

"That's true." Johnny agreed.

"This way we can be ourselves, we wouldn't be eating with our hands." I replied.

"I like your style Pam." Johnny said.

"Why thank you Sir." I chuckled.

"Here comes our pizza now."

"Johnny it doesn't bother me where we eat. I already have everything I want." I smiled.

"After we eat, I want to show you a place where my father use to take me after lunch." he said.

"You have another surprise. This is some night." I said.

"I know you'll like this place." he replied.

"I suppose you're not going to give me a clue." I assumed.

"You have that right. Why would I give away my surprise?" Johnny smiled.

"I was testing you, I thought maybe if I caught you off guard. . ."

"Well, you can forget it. I'm not going to tell you." he said.

"That's OK, I don't want to know, so what is it?" I asked.

"I thought you didn't want to know?"

"I was trying to trick you again." I said.

"You will have to wait." he demanded.

"Did I forget to mention that I have no patience?" I asked.

"That's funny you never did mention that."

"I'm not getting through to you am I."

"I'm not giving in." he said.

"I didn't think so." I smiled.

"The faster we eat the quicker we get there." Johnny said.

"You're right, let's take it with us." I said.

"You are right, you're very impatient." he declared.

"I tried telling you." I smiled.

"When we finish, we can go." he said.

"OK, I'll wait." I smiled. When we left the restaurant, Johnny ran into a candle store.

"I'll be only a moment." he said.

I didn't understand what Johnny was doing in a candle store. Was he buying candles? Johnny hurried out of the store so as not to keep me waiting.

"See Pam, it's a vanilla scented candle."

I didn't see the excitement in the candle.

"I bought this for when the candle is lit, our love will grow stronger. This candle will last forever just like our love."

I was shocked by Johnny's unbelievable words. I wanted to hear more on how he felt about us.

"Johnny, this night is very special to me you've made it perfect." I said.

"Pam, you're the only one here that's perfect." Johnny said.

"I have a pretty good catch myself." I smiled. I couldn't wait to see this special place Johnny was talking about. His face lit up just talking about it. We walked down a narrow path covered with long dried out grass. In its own way it was beautiful. There was a light up ahead. I assumed it was some sort of clearing.

I couldn't believe my eyes.

"Johnny this is amazing." I shouted.

"I knew you would like it." he said.

It was a crystal pond that rippled when the wind coasted across the top. All I could see was water the pond. It seemed to never end. The way the sun glittered through the trees made it a place I would never forget.

"My dad use to love this place." he said.

"Why did you stop going?" I asked.

"Things got better." he said.

Not understanding Johnny's reply I decided to ignore it. I didn't want to upset Johnny. We were having such a good time. What was he trying to say? I didn't understand what he meant. Things got better, what kind of an answer was that?

Johnny pulled the vanilla candle out from his pocket to light it. Then suddenly, what he said drifted from my mind as quickly as it entered. How could we feel alone again, as long as the flame from the candle burned in our hearts?

The ray from the candle felt warm against my finger tips. My whole body became warm with happiness. I wanted to hold onto this moment forever. Johnny laid out his jacket.

"Here, why don't you sit on this. I don't want you to get your pretty dress dirty." he said.

"Thank you very much." I said. The sun set through the trees in a shade of red. We sat by candlelight and I noticed Johnny put his head down. He was remembering why he use to come here. Gently I touched his hand.

"What's wrong Johnny?" I asked.

"I was remembering why my father and I use to

come here" Johnny stooped even lower.

"What is it?" I asked.

"When I was ten, my brother Henry died. He use to race cars."

"I'm sorry, Johnny." I said caringly.

"My mom and dad were always worried when he raced. I heard them say to him once, "Why don't you find something more secure?" He looked at them with distress on his face. He said, "I love what I do and if I have to die doing it, that is the way I want it to end." He explained how he was in his prime and nothing would ever happen to him. I always try to remember the words that he said. He'd rather die doing something he loved than be a failure for not even trying. My father would come down here to get away from his pain. In a way, it helped me too. I wish I could be as strong as Henry was." he said.

I slowly slipped my arm through his elbow. "Johnny you have many strengths." I encouraged.

"Why do you think I'm jealous of you? I'm afraid of losing you. I don't know why you're interested in me?" he said.

"Johnny, when I looked at you my life changed. I can't explain it, it's unbelievably powerful." I explained.

"See, you can't even tell me how you feel." Johnny shrugged.

"It's very hard for me to explain exactly how I feel." I said.

"Why can I tell you how I feel, you're kind, loving, you appreciate every thing I do, and I feel safe when I'm with you." he said.

"I can't explain how I feel I'm sorry."

"Maybe this relationship isn't worth my time."

Johnny shrugged.

"Johnny, a minute ago you were saying you were afraid to lose me and now you're leaving me." I shouted.

"I don't want to get too close to you if you don't know how you feel." he said.

"Johnny, we only have been out together on two dates." I said.

"I feel stronger for you than you do for me." Johnny explained.

"Johnny, I don't know what's going to happen. I know that I want to spend time with you." I said.

"That's not good enough for me!" Johnny yelled.

Johnny stood up and turned his back. I walked over. I slipped my hands around his stomach and squeezed him as tight as I could. Johnny's dense body suddenly lost all its strength. I didn't think Johnny could stay mad at me for long.

"Johnny we have to take it as it comes. I want to have an honest relationship and you're only forcing me to lie." I explained.

"You're right, I'm sorry everything was going so well. I didn't mean to ruin our evening." Johnny apologized.

"I'll know when I'm ready. I'll tell you my feelings." I said.

"I can get a little crazy at times." Johnny replied.

"Don't worry, so can I. You have been through a lot tonight, why don't you rest?" I suggested.

Johnny sat on the green grass that surrounded the quaint, comfortable pond. He looked very upset, as if something was eating him up inside. Even he didn't know what it was. All I could do was comfort him and to try to ease his pain. The sun went down. All you could see was Johnny and I by candlelight, filled with many dreams.

CHAPTER 10

"Pam, you have a phone call." Mom yelled.

"Mom, I'll be there in a minute." I said. When I answered the phone, I was surprised who it was.

"Hello"

"Hi, how is everything going?"

"Brad, is that really you?" I cried.

"Yes, it really is me." Brad said.

"What's up? Is there something wrong?" I asked.

"Everything's fine." he said.

"That's good." I replied.

"I was just calling to ask if you still have my baseball glove." Brad said.

Brad and I always played baseball in his neighborhood. It was always Jane, Samantha, Johnny and Johnny's brother Steve. We had such good times back then. I think we always lost against Johnny and Steve, they were really good. Sometimes we would even play touch football. I liked that game the best.

"Sure, I put it in my trunk the other day." I replied.

"Is there anyway that I could come and pick it

up sometime?" Brad asked.

"I could drop it off for you if you'd like." I suggested.

"That would be great it will save me the trip." Brad thanked.

"I'll be down, in an hour to drop it off." I said.

"That's great! I really appreciate it." Brad said.

"It's no problem at all." It was going to be very hard for me to see Brad again. It's been awhile. I wonder if I will still have feelings for him. If I do remember what it use to be like with Brad then I will never want to go back to him. Johnny's nice, he thinks of me, he's never selfish or mean in anyway. I must keep remembering that when I see Brad. I know it's going to be very hard for me. It always is when you see someone you use to date especially, when you had strong feelings for that person. I'll get through it by thinking about Johnny and how special he is to me.

When I arrived, Brad was on the porch waiting for me. He looked really well, he had on decent clothes. I looked at Brad and many fond memories came rushing back. There was no doubt about it I missed him. I couldn't erase all the memories we once shared. I wish I could date both of them. I knew I could never do that it wasn't fair. It was difficult sneaking around with Johnny, Brad didn't even know.

"Here's the glove you wanted." I smiled.

"Thanks, why don't you sit for a minute and talk about old times?" Brad asked.

I sat down, I don't know maybe I really did want to be with Brad. Maybe I knew this could be the last day we'd ever spend together.

"You're taking care of yourself, you look really well" Brad said.

"Yeah, I exercise every day." I said.

"That's really good keep up the good work." Brad replied.

"Oh I will if I want to keep this figure I have to exercise every day." I laughed. It was good talking to Brad as a friend we never really talked like this before. I liked it. We were getting along great. I was amazed! I couldn't get too comfortable, because it would never be like this again.

"What have you been doing lately?" I asked.

"You're not going to believe it. I got a job working down at the lumber yard." Brad said.

"That's great how do you like it?" I asked.

"It's really fun at times I enjoy working with the people." Brad said.

I lost track of time sitting there with Brad. I could have sat there all day. He was a pleasure to be around since we were not dating. All the pressure was off and we had nothing to worry about, it was great!

"I see you returned more than just my baseball glove." he said.

"Yeah, I figured you might have wanted these things." I replied.

"My Yankee's baseball hat! I remember when you first tried it on. You looked so beautiful." Brad smiled.

"I remember it was the first time we played baseball and I stole it from you." I laughed.

"The good old days all seemed so simple." Brad thought.

"You're right things were simpler then." I said.

"I guess we grew up." Brad said.

"Maybe we could have stayed younger instead of growing up so fast." I said.

"That's true." Brad agreed.

I saw something black coming around the corner. I turned my head to look, it was Johnny's black Mustang. Maybe he won't notice, I hoped he didn't see us sitting up here. My car was in the driveway. I didn't think he would say anything in front of Brad, it was a big secret. Johnny would never do that. He knew how I felt about Brad. Johnny wasn't going to like this, Brad and I sitting together on his porch. I could see Johnny didn't have a good expression on his face when he saw my car in the driveway.

"Oh Pam, look over there it's Johnny. Maybe he would like to join us. I'm sure he would be glad to see you." Brad said.

"Oh, yeah really glad." I muttered.

"Hey Johnny why don't you come and join us we were just talking about old times." Brad said.

Johnny walked over slowly you could tell he was ready to explode with anger. His fists were clenched tightly and his head hung low. I was afraid Johnny was going to say something. Johnny didn't look like he could hold it inside much longer.

"Johnny what are you doing out of work so early?" I asked.

"Why, is this what you two do when I am at work?" Johnny assumed. Johnny was going to blow it. I knew he couldn't handle keeping this a secret. It was going to ruin everything. I hoped Brad didn't know what he was talking about.

"Johnny always comes home for lunch. Pam you forgot, remember when we use to play baseball?" Brad asked.

"I wished I'd remembered that." I muttered.

Good, Brad had no idea about Johnny's questions he must have thought he was kidding around.

"Pam, what do you think you're doing? Is this what you do while I'm at work?" Johnny said angrily.

"What's going on?" Brad asked.

"Pam, I told you not to see him." Johnny yelled.

"I knew it! I should have known you two had a thing together." Brad yelled.

"It's not like that at all Brad!" I cried.

"Pam just tell the truth." Johnny smirked.

"Johnny you know it's not like this." I screamed.

"Brad you stay out of this if you know what's good for you." Johnny smirked.

"Johnny!" I yelled.

"Brad, don't go let me explain." I pleaded.

"Pam you don't owe him any explanation let's go!" Johnny shouted.

"Johnny wait!" I screamed.

"I knew you would go running back to him. What now I can't please you, what about the beach? Pam, don't you remember that?" Johnny sighed. Johnny got into his car and drove off screeching his tires.

"What's going on out here?" Brad's mom asked.

"Mom, we're only talking you should get inside." Brad replied.

"Come on Pam let's take a walk." Brad suggested.

"Brad I'm sorry about Johnny." I apologized.

"You don't have to apologize for him." he said.

"I wish some how things didn't have to end like this." I said.

"It's too bad, it does have to happen." he replied.

"Johnny was there to pick up the broken pieces for me he's been a big help." I said.

"Things could have been different if we just did

more things. We always had trouble expressing ourselves." Brad said.

"Yeah, I remember." I replied.

"Where do we go from here?" Brad asked.

"We smile, hug each other and move on. You know we don't work together." I said.

"You're right, good-bye Pam." Brad sighed.

"Good-bye Brad." Brad and I gave a friendly hug and I kissed him on the cheek. It was an emotional moment. Tears rolled from our eyes as we embraced. We knew it was for the best and we knew it would be hard to let go. I hugged him for a long time hoping to take away some of his pain. Whenever I was feeling blue, Brad would hold me really tight. He'd shake me up and down and say, "You shake all the bad stuff right out of there."

I wish it were that easy. My memories of Brad would never go away. I will never forget Brad he was a big part of my life and he always would be. Your mind never lets you forget.

Later, at work Johnny's mother stopped by.

"I was wondering if you would like to come over for supper tonight?" she asked.

"Sure I would love to, thank you very much." I replied.

"I heard so much about you. I thought it was time for me to meet you." she said.

"What time would you like me to arrive?" I asked.

"How about seven or even earlier if you want." she said.

"Seven is fine." I replied.

"OK, I'll see you then." Johnny's mother said.

"It was nice meeting you."

There was only one problem. Johnny wasn't

talking to me. After going over Brads' house he might never talk to me again. He should understand that Brad and my relationship was over. He must think I have no feelings for him. Besides, Brad would see me having dinner with Johnny's family. He and I always had dinner with his family. We went to many restaurants together. After Brad and I settled everything he would have to see me again. It will never end. In the spring I probably will be sitting on Johnny's porch. His sister Kate, Diana and baby Mary too. Brad will surely see me then, there is no way out. Brad and I will just have to deal with it. If Johnny wasn't Brad's next door neighbor I wouldn't have this problem, it would be a lot easier. I had an idea, I would walk to Johnny's house it's not far only a couple blocks up the road.

When I got there, Johnny was already home from work.

"Hello, I'm glad you could make it." Johnny's mother said.

"It's a pleasure." I said.

"Honey, I want you to meet Pam." Johnny's mother said.

"Hi it's nice to finally meet you." Johnny's father said.

"It's nice meeting you." I replied. Johnny's dad and I sat at the table while Johnny's mother served the meal.

"Johnny, we have a guest for dinner." His mom yelled.

Johnny came out with his head down. He didn't look very well. He must have been coming down with something. Johnny saw me at the table. He was surely surprised to see that I was the dinner guest. Johnny put his head back down, pulled out his chair and slammed it down making a long tinging noise. He then slammed his body into the chair. Johnny's parents looked at each other confused.

"If I knew it was going to be Pam, I would not have come out." Johnny smirked.

"Johnny stop it!" His mother yelled.

"May I please be excused?" Johnny asked. Johnny got up from the table.

"Would you please excuse me?" I asked.

"Sure go right ahead." Johnny's dad said.

"Don't come near me Pam. Why don't you go sit with Brad somewhere how about his porch?" Johnny yelled.

I followed Johnny upstairs to his room.

"It must be jealousy, that's funny he was never jealous of his other girlfriends." Johnny's mother said.

"You know what that means, he's in love with her. I was jealous of you too and I married you, it runs in the family." Johnny's dad said.

"That's true, I'm sure she didn't do anything wrong. He's just accusing her like you use to do to me." Johnny's mother smiled.

"You're probably right I'm sure that's exactly what he's doing he is my son." Johnny's dad said.

I was trying to calm Johnny down, but he wouldn't listen. "Johnny, nothing happened!" I cried.

"Pam like you would tell me if something did!" Johnny yelled.

"Yes I would our relationship is based on the truth." I shouted.

"What relationship, you think we have one?" Johnny smirked.

"Johnny do you really feel that way?" I asked.

"No, I just felt like saying that." Johnny smirked.

"After everything I gave up for you!" I cried.

"What did you give up for me? I was the one who had to see you and Brad kissing in the car. I was the one who saw you going out places and swimming together. You wrote me a letter saying you left Brad. You were just trying to keep me on a string. You were sure you wouldn't fall and Johnny the little puppet would be there to catch you." Johnny yelled.

"Johnny what do you want me to do? I can't take it back and if you can't forgive me that's fine." I screamed.

"Yeah, that's what you want. You don't want to hurt my feelings when you go back to Brad." Johnny snarled.

"I'm not going back to Brad. How did I know you even liked me? You wrote me a letter saying it wasn't right. Was I supposed to take that as yes you liked me? I had no idea you had feelings for me." I explained.

"Try to talk your way out of it, it won't work. Just get out of here!" Johnny shouted.

I put my head down and walked down stairs.

"I'm really sorry I ruined your dinner." I apologized.

"You're welcome to stay if you'd like." Johnny's mother offered.

"No thanks, I don't think Johnny wants me here." I explained.

"You must come back again." she said.

"I don't think I can, I'm sorry." I said.

"We really enjoyed having you here I'm sure we'll see you again." she said.

"Thank you." I said. I left hurt and upset. I knew Johnny would never call me again the relationship I thought would last forever was gone. I never forgot that warm summer day we spent on the beach with the seagulls over head and the sound of the waves crashing along the shore.

"Johnny I wouldn't let that young woman go you can tell she loves you very much." Johnny's dad said.

"You don't understand." Johnny explained.

"I'm afraid I do understand. I was the same way with your mother if she looked at another man. I was a man-eating shark ready for the kill. I love your mother. She's the only woman I love." Johnny's father explained.

"You better go after her son." Johnny's mother said.

"Once you find someone you can't let them go. You have to hold on as tight as you can that's why your mother and I have been married thirty years." Johnny's dad explained.

Johnny ran out the door hoping he could catch up with me before I went home.

"Pam wait!" Johnny yelled.

I turned around, Johnny was running toward me. I stopped. Johnny caught up to me pretty fast. He stopped and took me into his arms.

"I'm sorry, I should have trusted you." Johnny apologized.

Johnny's lips touched mine and his arms wrapped around me so snug. It was like he didn't want to ever let me go. I held him tight. I wanted him to know I forgave him.

"I'm sorry. I need you please don't leave me." Johnny pleaded.

"Johnny, everything is going to be all right." I

tried to comfort him.

"I'm afraid to get hurt." Johnny muttered. Johnny sank his head into my chest.

"Johnny I don't think you understand. You were the one I wanted. Every time you saw Brad and I kissing, I wanted to be kissing you. I really tried not to do things with Brad. I didn't want you to see us together. Somehow you always came home at the wrong time. I need you just as much as you need me." I explained.

"It's hard with him living next door. I have to see him every day all that does is trigger memories of you and him together. When I turned the corner and saw you sitting together on the porch laughing I couldn't help but think it was all starting over. Maybe you can't feel what I feel." he said.

Johnny and I sat along the curb to talk things over.

"Johnny I know how you feel. I spent many days and nights at Brad's house waiting for you to come home. If I could just see you I was happy. I would stare out the window watching and listening for your car. My ears were tuned into the sound of your car. I would always try to get everybody out onto the porch. That was the only way I could see you. Jane always liked sitting out there and most of the time Brad wouldn't come out. I could see you and spend less time with Brad. There was one night I should have never been out on that porch. It was late, I stayed at Brads until one in the morning. You weren't home yet. You came home to drop your car off and waiting for you was a young woman with long red hair. I was so upset with you that woman should have been me in the car not her. I knew it would never be me. I was really surprised to see you with another woman. That's when I decided to give up. It wasn't worth all this pain. I wanted you more than anything. I knew I had to stop right there or I could never get on with my life. There was a time when I left Brad just to get away from the both of you. I wanted to start over. I spent most of my nights down the cape to think things out. I knew I couldn't have both of you. I met someone down the cape, but it wasn't you Johnny. I thought I could fulfill this strong void, but it didn't work. He could never have taken the place of you. It only lasted three days. I tried to like him. He told me he wasn't interested in me. It was easy to see why I couldn't get over you Johnny. He thought I was in love with him. My brother thought that was funny, he knew I could never love someone like him. I told him I wasn't interested in him. He knew who I was interested in. I knew I could only love one man and that's you Johnny my true love. I knew I couldn't see anyone. At least not until I got over you or gave it time for Brad and my relationship to cool off. I figured you would realize I wanted you and not Brad. I had no intention of ever going back to Brad. I always knew what I wanted. To think I still have strong feelings for you after all this time." I explained.

Johnny lifted his head from staring at the ground.

"That's really how you felt all this time?" Johnny asked.

"Yes, I never dreamed we would ever be together. When you told me to get out of your house, that hurt. I understand you were mad." I said.

"I know I was mad, I should have never treated you that way. My temper gets the best of me sometimes." Johnny apologized.

"I forgive you. I would never risk losing you over this." I said.

"The same goes for me." Johnny smiled.

"This thing with Brad will pass. You won't think of me and Brad together. You'll think of me and you. There were times I wished I never dated Brad. Then you would have dated me right away. Then, I thought if I never met Brad I wouldn't have met you. That would have been a worse price to pay not having you." I said.

Johnny held me tight I think now he understands how I felt all this time. It was really tough being away from him. I had to be sure what I wanted or I would have been doing the same thing to Johnny as I did to Brad. I never wanted to go through that again. There was never much doubt in my mind. I didn't want Johnny to know how I felt. I had the shakes. I was feeling nauseous in the morning.

Barely being able to talk when I saw him, was definitely a case of love. I knew it was love, because I never felt this strong for anyone. The feelings I thought I felt for Brad weren't the same as those I felt for Johnny.

"Why don't we go to my house and eat that terrific supper my mother went through all that trouble to cook?" Johnny said.

"Let's go! They'll be happy we're going to eat." I smiled. Johnny took my hand and we walked home.

"I'm glad we patched things up. I was a little nervous there for a minute." Johnny smiled.

"You were nervous, I was dying." I said.

"We will be a hundred years old and you'll be saying you threw me out." Johnny laughed.

"You're really pushing your luck today." I smiled.

We were back to our old selves again, until we saw Brad outside.

"Oh no I was hoping he wouldn't see us together." I said.

"I think it's too late for that don't you?" he said.

"Yeah a little, now he's looking at us together, you must know how that feels Johnny."

"I surely do! I felt it long enough." Johnny turned to me and made a face.

"You better watch your step mister if you know what's good for you." I laughed.

"Hey what's up Brad?" Johnny asked.

"Not much Johnny." Brad replied.

Johnny walked over toward Brad. I think Johnny was trying to rub it in Brad's face that we were together. Brad and I just stared at each other.

"I am sorry about what happened today." Johnny apologized.

"That's cool. I don't want to stand in the way of you two." Brad said.

"I'm really glad you see it that way Brad." Johnny said.

I wasn't saying anything it wasn't my place. If I did Johnny would probably give me a dirty look. To save myself embarrassment and a fight I kept my mouth shut.

Then Brad started talking to me. "Pam do you remember the time we went down the Cape. We danced all night till our feet hurt then in the morning we took an early swim." Brad smiled.

Johnny was going to hit the roof. I didn't know what Johnny was going to do. Now his face was bright red.

"I think I'll go inside the house now." I said.

"Yeah, you better go inside. I wouldn't want you to see Johnny get hurt." Brad said.

"Stay right here don't even move. I don't want you to miss this." Johnny smirked.

I really didn't want to see Johnny and Brad fight. I didn't want to see any one get hurt. It wasn't fair that Johnny was going to make me watch this.

"What's the matter Pam, Johnny has you under control? He doesn't own you!" Brad said angrily.

"Brad, why don't you keep your mouth shut." Johnny yelled. Johnny was furious, this was it. He was never going to talk to me again and I didn't even say anything. I tried not to get involved, but it looked like Brad involved me all by himself. I didn't dare answer him. Johnny would have ripped my head off. What was he going to do to Brad and why did I have to watch? I didn't want to see two people I had feelings for shedding blood. I couldn't stop them Johnny would think I was sticking up for Brad. I might as well dive into a tank with ten hungry sharks covered with blood. I decided to back up slowly edging my way toward Johnny's house.

"I knew I should have never introduced you to each other. If I had it to do over you two would have never met." Brad angered.

I had to defend myself and Johnny.

"That's not true if it wasn't Johnny it would had been someone else." I screamed.

"See, Johnny! It would have been someone else. You were just there." Brad yelled.

"What are you trying to say Pam?" Johnny snapped.

"You know what I mean."

"No, sorry I don't." Johnny snared.

"Johnny does it really matter? I fell in love with you!" I explained.

"Now, I'm not so sure. I was just there remember you would have fallen in love with someone else?" Johnny yelled.

"How could I love someone else, I love you?" I pleaded.

"Did you say that to Brad too?" Johnny asked.

"Yes she did." Brad smirked.

"Johnny you're not going to believe him are you?" I asked.

"Maybe I should." Johnny muttered.

"Johnny maybe there wouldn't have been anyone else." I said.

"That isn't what you told me. You said he was just there to pick up the pieces." Brad smiled.

"Johnny, I said that before, but now I know you better." I explained.

"Pam, you told me that yesterday. Just one day and you know him better, that's hard to believe." Brad laughed.

I knew I was in trouble. What was I going to say to Johnny to get out of this? We had such an honest relationship. I couldn't lie now, he could probably tell.

"I only said that to make Brad feel better." I said.

"See Brad, a perfectly good explanation." Johnny smirked.

"She really knows how to cover up and you believe her. She lied to me all the time." Brad said.

"We happen to have an honest relationship." Johnny remarked.

"Oh, did she tell you that too?" Brad yelled.

"No, that was my idea." Johnny replied.

That's when Johnny realized Brad was lying.

He was only trying to get us into a fight. He wanted more than anything to split us up for good. Even if I didn't take him back. He had no idea Johnny's and my relationship was build on trust.

"Brad, it's not going to happen. I love Pam, I'm not going to treat her like you did." Johnny explained.

"You love me?" I asked. Johnny looked at me and smiled.

"Of course I love you." Johnny replied.

"I never heard you say it before." I said.

"I love you." Johnny said.

"Oh, please give me a tissue could we get on with this?" Brad smirked.

"Brad who asked you?" Johnny yelled.

"You two love each other that's a joke, she once loved me too." Brad said.

"Brad, don't try to equal our relationship to yours!" Johnny yelled.

"You're right our relationship lasted three years, yours won't last more than two weeks." Brad snapped.

"Brad, I'm getting really sick of your smart comments." Johnny angered.

"Johnny, is that all you could come up with to say, how original." Brad said.

"Gee Brad, I thought you were cruel when I dated you, now I really see how much of a jerk you are." I said.

"Oh Pam, I'm so disappointed." Brad said.

"I'm glad you left me!" I shouted.

"Wait a minute I thought you left him?" Johnny asked.

"I did for a week then we started seeing each other again, but it didn't work out." I explained.

"That's really nice of you to tell me." Johnny

said.

"You never asked." I replied.

"We wouldn't be standing here right now would we?" Johnny asked.

"Johnny I really don't know. I can't predict what would happen. If I had left again I knew I wasn't happy. I believed in working things out." I explained.

Johnny turned his back and walked away. Watching him leave hurt my insides. I let the one thing in my life turn his back on me. What was I supposed to say to him? I'm not really good at comforting someone I never know what to say. I don't think I should have let him go like that. He must think I don't care about him. I have trouble expressing my feelings. If I didn't always hide behind a wall, maybe people would know what I'm really like. Instead I make up someone else that people would like. I'm afraid they won't like the real person. What am I going to do knock on the door? He and his parents are probably not talking to me now, especially if Johnny told them what happened. I had the man of my dreams and I lost him.

CHAPTER 11

"Beep, Beep."

"Johnny, I have to pick up my sister at the roller skating rink." Timmy said. Timmy was Johnny's side kick they've been friends since elementary school he was always able to get Johnny to do things.

"Where is the rink?" Johnny asked.

"Canton." Timmy said.

They looked around the roller skating rink trying to find Timmy's sister. Johnny started to laugh.

"We are definitely not going to find any babes in here." Johnny chuckled.

"Except for her!" Timmy exclaimed.

She was a young woman with shoulder length blonde hair, long legs and a short skirt.

"Johnny, we could go over there and ask her to join us." Timmy suggested.

The young woman looked over at the two boys and smiled.

"Timmy that's my girlfriend Pam I wonder what she is doing here?" Johnny smirked.

"Sorry I had no idea." Timmy apologized.

"Either did I." Johnny muttered.

"Hi Johnny." I said.

"Pam, what are you doing here?" Johnny asked.

"What are you doing here picking up what's the word, "babes"?" I laughed.

"Pam, I'm serious I asked you a question." Johnny angered.

"I'm picking up my niece and nephew they come here every Saturday." I said.

"They must know my sister Darine?" Timmy asked.

"Oh yes, they talk about her all the time." I said.

"My name's Timmy."

"Mine's Pam, it's really a pleasure to meet you." I said.

"Why don't you two run off and get married?" Johnny smirked.

"Johnny please we just met, maybe tomorrow." I laughed.

"Johnny we were only talking." Timmy explained.

"Well a minute ago you were drooling over her." Johnny said.

"Johnny I would never do that to you." Timmy said.

"You don't know Pam. Pam, you're not going to write him a letter like you did for me are you?" Johnny smirked.

"Would you excuse us for a minute?" I asked.

"Sure go right ahead." Timmy said.

"Thank you." I quickly pulled Johnny's arm to a quiet spot to talk. "Excuse me what was that all about you embarrassed me." I said.

"Why, am I hurting your chances with Tim?"

Johnny smirked.

"What are you talking about?" I said.

"I saw the way you looked at him. You looked like a lion watching its prey." he said.

"How did I look at him? There's a certain way now?" I shouted.

"Yeah, there's a look! The one where you look him up and down!" Johnny yelled.

"I did not Johnny! Johnny I love you, but I surely don't think you understand." I yelled. I stomped out of the roller skating rink in a fit of rage. I couldn't believe him, a look he's crazy. Now he'll probably make me wear a paper bag over my head so I will not look at people. I can't stop living my life because he thinks I look at his friends the wrong way. What am I supposed to do put my head down when I'm talking? He probably doesn't want me to talk either. I'll have a piece of tape over my mouth and a bag over my head if we ever go out again.

Later that evening I heard a knock at the door.

"Timmy what are you doing here?" I asked.

"Johnny wanted me to give you this." Timmy explained.

"Thanks Timmy." I said. Timmy handed me a white envelope. I was afraid to even open the white envelope that I now had possession of. What if he doesn't want to see me anymore after my performance at the skating rink? I hope he doesn't think I like Timmy. He's nice, but not my type. Margo would love Timmy I'll have to set them up if Johnny and I are still talking. I slowly pealed the seal on the envelope and pulled out the small folded piece of white paper.

Dear Pam,

Meet me at our favorite place.

Love, Johnny

P.S. It's wet and sandy.

Of course, I knew what favorite place. Johnny was talking about the beach. The place where we had our first date, the place where all the magic began. I never want to be apart from Johnny. Things were much easier when we would sit there alone and talk. The waves would soothe our minds to only concentrate on each other. If only we could get that all back. Johnny must be waiting for me I'll have to leave now I thought.

It was getting late there weren't many people on the beach. I walked to the spot where Johnny and I first sat. That's were Johnny was, sitting on a blanket. A vase full of roses, one white candle and a light brown bag with something I did not know what was inside.

"I was afraid you wouldn't show." Johnny said.

"It never crossed my mind." I smiled.

"What made you want to come?" he asked.

"I figured I would have a good time with or without you." I laughed.

"OK, you know what I have to do, tickle you." Johnny smiled.

"Oh no." I chuckled. I took off towards the water trying to get away from Johnny. Johnny and I were running across the beach like the first time. Maybe it's possible we could patch things up.

The way our hands fit so tight together. The sand

was between our toes and the water splashed against our ankles, it was perfect. I was in love all over again. We walked for an hour enjoying eachothers company.

"Pam come on, I'll race you." he said.

Johnny and I ran toward the blanket and we both fell down. Johnny grabbed the brown bag.

"I brought you my specialty." Johnny chuckled.

Johnny pulled out two cinnamon rolls and two orange juices. It was the first breakfast we ate together. Johnny was truly amazing I could never stay mad at him for long. He always knew how to make things better. Every time I looked at Johnny everything seemed to fade. You could get lost in his eyes.

I would have missed out on so many things if I stayed with Brad. I didn't know what life was until I met Johnny. I can't look back and say I wish I met Johnny first. I think the reason I appreciate Johnny as much as I do is because Brad was mean. With Johnny I would have gotten spoiled and I know I would have taken him for granted. Now, I can appreciate him. Johnny definitely deserves someone to enjoy his special charm. Nobody should settle for someone that treats you the wrong way. There isn't a person in the world that should be treated wrong. If you always have someone putting you down you slowly die inside. There's nothing left but your empty shell.

CHAPTER 12

I sat at the table for hours thinking about something special to do for Johnny. A few things came to mind, but nothing that grabbed my attention. It was really important for him to have fun. For him to know that I've appreciated everything he has done for me. Then finally an idea clicked, I had to get started right away. I have to write Johnny a letter. I'm afraid if I saw him I would give the whole surprise away.

Dear Johnny,

Meet me down by old Zummers field at 7:00. I have a surprise for you.

Love,
Pam

My hands were shaking and my knees felt weak. Pacing back and forth waiting for Johnny I wanted everything to be perfect. Everything he has done for me, I had to make it very special. I never really knew how much of a special person Johnny can be. He's sweet, kind and charming all in one. There's one thing he can always get me to do, smile. Sometimes when I look at him and smile, I know how lucky I really am. I don't think anything could ever come between me and Johnny. He's the only one that ever thought of me in a long time.

"Johnny, I'm over here." I yelled. Johnny came running over with a small gift wrapped in light pink paper with red ribbon.

"Hi Pam, I got you something special. I hope you like it." Johnny said.

"I like anything you give me Johnny." I quickly unwrapped the paper dying to find out what was inside.

"Oh Johnny, it's beautiful. I love it!" I exclaimed. Inside the red velvet box was a gold chain with a charm of a gold rose. I embraced Johnny tightly.

"Thank you very much." I praised.

"Turn around Pam, let me put it on." Johnny suggested.

"Look at it Johnny the way it shines when the sun hits it just right." I said.

"Pam you're the one that makes that necklace beautiful you give it a certain glow." Johnny smiled.

"Johnny you're the kindest person. I'm never going to take this off. Now every time I look in the mirror I'll think of you. Whenever I feel alone I can hold it tight in my hand and I'll never be lonely again."

Johnny reached over and gave me a soft kiss on the cheek. "Thank you Pam I needed to hear that." Johnny smiled.

"Now for your surprise close your eyes." I grabbed and pulled him under a tree. Under the tree I laid out a blanket. I brought a picnic basket filled with chicken, rolls, chocolate cake and of course the famous cinnamon roll and orange juice. I lit the white candle Johnny bought me. We always light it when we're together, just like Johnny promised. Days were getting shorter. There never seemed to be enough time to spend with Johnny. All the time we spend together we try to make it special.

"You're always doing special things for me. I had to repay you in some sort of way." I said.

"You didn't have to do all this. I like writing you letters and creating surprises you're worth all my effort." he said.

"I didn't want you to think I receive without giving." I replied.

"You gave plenty. Yourself that's all I ever needed." Johnny said.

"I still felt I had to repay you, remember when I told you I would tell you how I felt when I was ready? I'm ready and this is how I express myself, by doing something nice for you." I replied.

"I already know how you feel I can see it." Johnny smiled.

"Now we both feel the same way about each other not like before." I said.

"I don't think so. I'll always love you more." Johnny chuckled.

"OK, I'm never doing anything nice for you again." I joked.

"I really appreciate you going through all this trouble for me." he said.

"Then it was worth it, but the fun is only beginning." I said.

"What do you have planned for me?" Johnny asked.

"I can't tell you."

When Johnny looked through the trees he saw two beautiful brown horses grazing in the meadow.

"Look Pam! Do you see those two horses out there? Johnny exclaimed.

"I know."

"That's my surprise? I can't believe it!"

"Believe it I bought them for us. I figured this would be a good place to escape and we could bring them to the pond that you like." I said.

"Pam, do they have names?" he asked.

"Montey is yours and mine's Carolina I think they're in love. You can tell how they look at each other." I chuckled.

"Why, are we sitting here let's go see them." he said.

"Johnny I couldn't afford to buy saddles, but I'll show you how to ride a horse bare back. I use to ride that way when I was a kid."

"I'll try anything once." he said.

"All you have to do is hold onto the mane and lock your feet tight against the horses stomach." I explained.

"It doesn't sound too hard." Johnny replied.

"Let me help you." I said.

"Wow this is great. I'm on top of the world." Johnny shouted.

"I must say you do look a lot taller." After I helped Johnny get on his horse I quickly hopped on mine.

"Johnny you're not going to have much control over the horse Make sure you hold on tight." I coached.

"Don't worry about me. I don't even care if I fall off this is going to be fun." he said.

I smiled at Johnny, watching him was the best present he could have given me.

"I feel just like a cowboy."

"Hey Johnny, I'll race you."

Being here with Johnny was a dream I never wanted to wake up from. It was great the way we rode across the green meadow with the sun setting low. It felt too good to be true I wondered if life with Johnny would always be this good. We're still young and we have a lot more things to see together. Someday Johnny and I are going to see the world.